Rob Scotton

Russell

the
Sheep

HarperCollins *Children's Books*

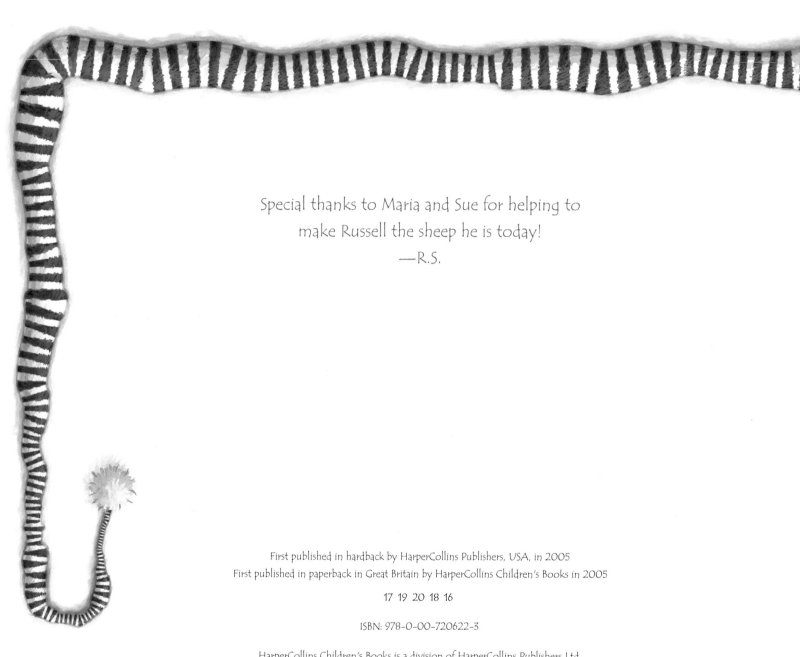

Special thanks to Maria and Sue for helping to
make Russell the sheep he is today!
—R.S.

First published in hardback by HarperCollins Publishers, USA, in 2005
First published in paperback in Great Britain by HarperCollins Children's Books in 2005

17 19 20 18 16

ISBN: 978-0-00-720622-3

HarperCollins Children's Books is a division of HarperCollins Publishers Ltd.
Text and illustrations copyright © Rob Scotton 2005
Typography by Martha Rago

Visit our website at www.harpercollins.co.uk

Printed and bound by Printing Express, Hong Kong

www.robscotton.com

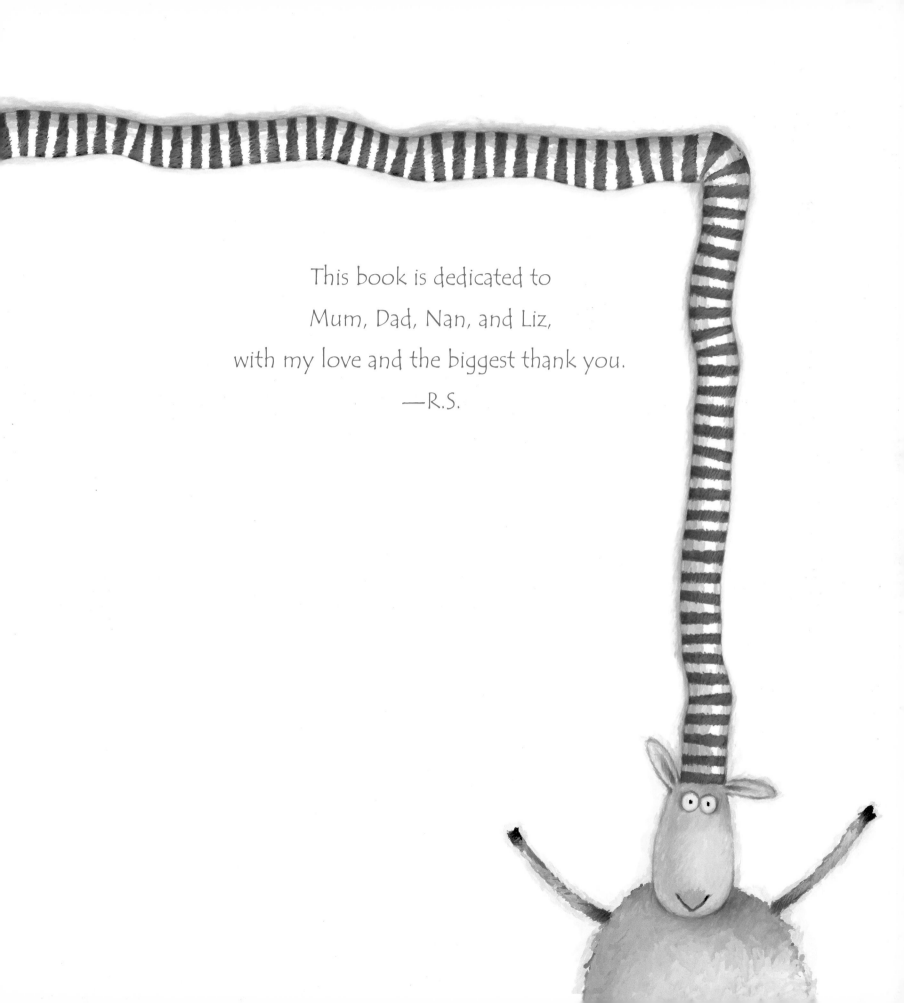

This book is dedicated to
Mum, Dad, Nan, and Liz,
with my love and the biggest thank you.
—R.S.

Russell the sheep lived in Frogsbottom Field.

At the end of a long busy day...

...night fell and the sheep got ready for bed.

Soon all was quiet.

Except for...

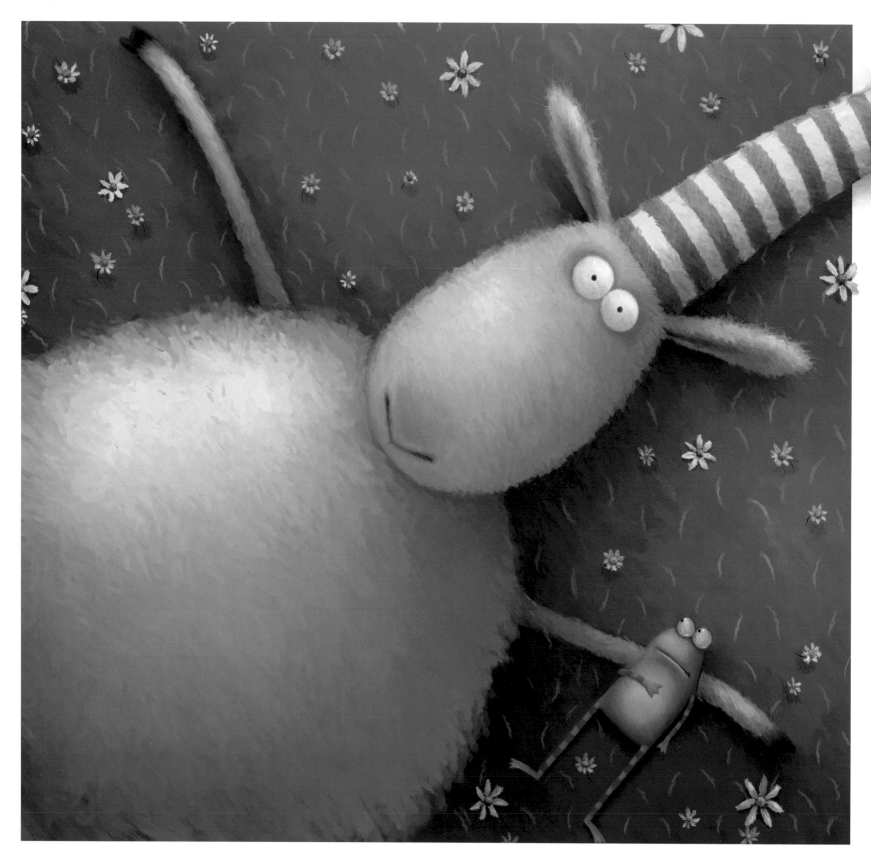

No matter how hard he tried, Russell could not fall asleep.

"Maybe if it were really dark," he thought, "I'd be able to sleep."

But the really dark really scared him.

"Perhaps I'm too hot," he thought.

"Perhaps I'm not."

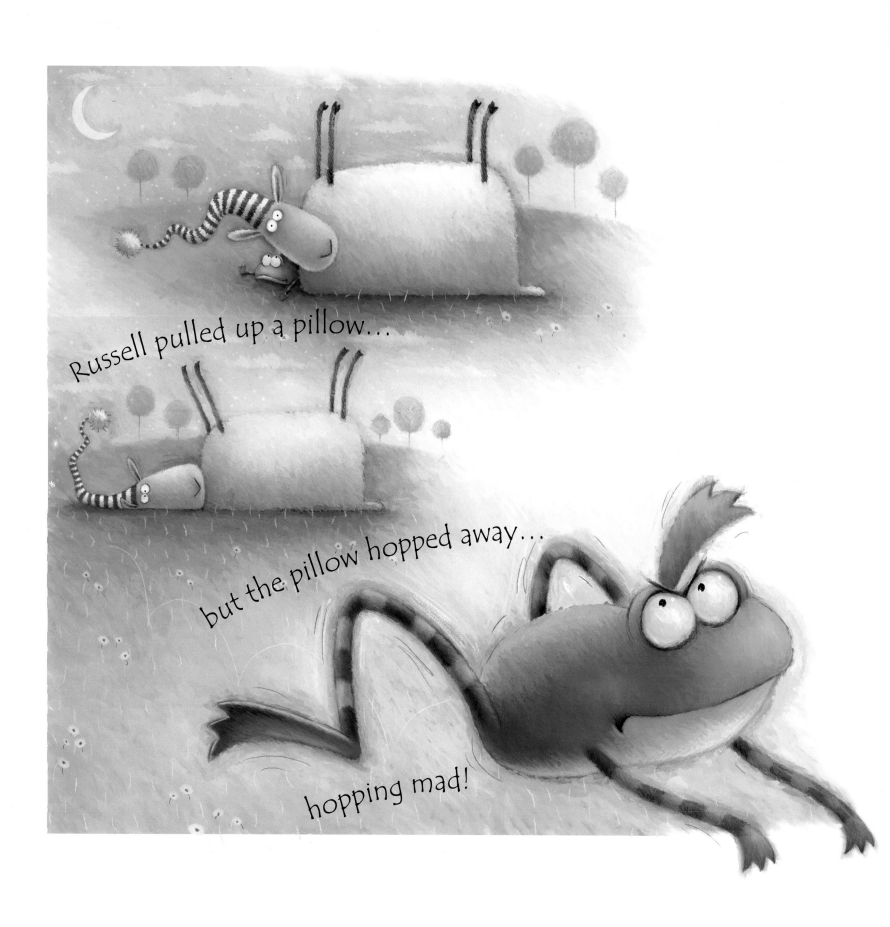

Russell pulled up a pillow…

but the pillow hopped away…

hopping mad!

"Maybe I need a better place to sleep," he decided, and went for a walk.

Russell spied the boot of the rusty car.

It was **too** cramped!

He tried the hollow of a tree.

That was **too creepy!**

Russell even tried sleeping on a branch.

But it was too crowded!

WHAT'S A SHEEP TO DO?

Russell thought he would never get to sleep. But then he had a brilliant idea.

What if he tried to count things? That would make him fall asleep.

Russell counted his feet.

One…

two…

three…

four.

Not tired.

"Hmmm. I guess I need more feet," he decided.

"What next?"

The stars! Russell counted each and every one.

One...two...three...four...five...

six hundred million billion and ten.

And Russell was wide awake!

He counted them again…

six hundred million billion and ten!

And still wide awake!

Russell thought very hard.

In fact, he thought so hard, his hat went ziggy-zaggy!

"I know," he shouted. "I'll count sheep!"

One...

two...

three...four...five...

six...

seven…eight…

nine…

"Still awake," he said and sighed.

Then Russell realised he had forgotten
to count one very important little sheep…

...himself!

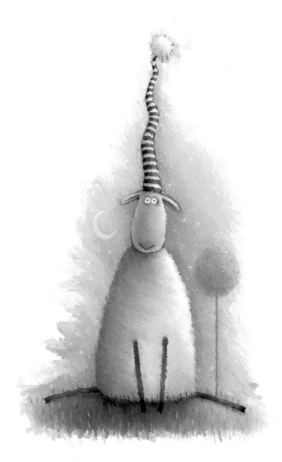

"Ten!"

Russell felt a tickle, then a twitch, and then…

…sound asleep.

By now it was morning, and all the other sheep in the field began getting ready for the new day.

Soon everyone was up. Everyone that is, except for...

...Russell.